My Wild Woolly

My Wild Woolly

Deborah J. Eaton
Illustrated by G. Brian Karas

Green Light Readers
Harcourt, Inc.
Orlando Austin New York San Diego Toronto London

"Mom," I said.
"There's a Wild Woolly in
the yard."

But Mom said, "There is no Wild Woolly in the yard. Go out and play. Have a good time."

I climbed a tree.
The Wild Woolly climbed the tree, too.

I played ball.
The Wild Woolly played ball, too.

I ate a peanut butter sandwich.
The Wild Woolly ate a peanut butter
sandwich, too.

That night, I climbed into bed. "There is no Wild Woolly in the yard," said Mom. "Right?"

"Right," I said.
"He's under my bed!"

What's My

Goodness gracious me!
What animal can this be?

My animal is brown
It has four legs. It has
pointy nose. It has a
fluffy tail.

A Wild Woolly is a
make-believe animal.
Can you draw a picture
of a *real* animal?

Animal?

1. Draw a picture of an animal. Do not show it to anyone!

2. Ask a friend to guess what it is. Give some clues.

Is it a fox?

Pet Peek-Over Bookmarks

The boy in the story had a Wild Woolly as a pet.

What kind of pet would you like to have?

Here's a way to make a bookmark with your favorite pet peeking over the top.

You can write what you know about that pet inside!

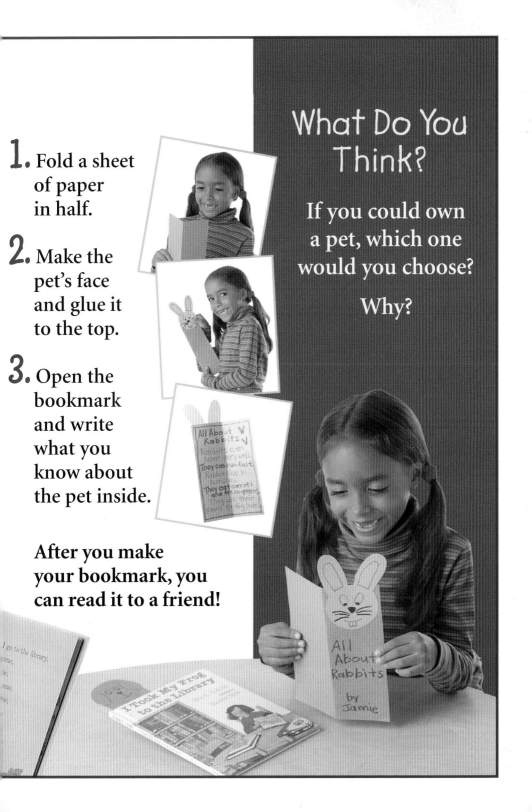

1. Fold a sheet of paper in half.

2. Make the pet's face and glue it to the top.

3. Open the bookmark and write what you know about the pet inside.

After you make your bookmark, you can read it to a friend!

What Do You Think?

If you could own a pet, which one would you choose?

Why?

Meet the Illustrator

G. Brian Karas enjoyed painting the pictures in this book. He has a "Wild Woolly" of his own at home—a fluffy dog named Otto!

Requests for permission to make copies of any part of the work should be mailed
to the following address: Permissions Department, Harcourt, Inc.,
6277 Sea Harbor Drive, Orlando, Florida 32887-6777.

www.HarcourtBooks.com

First Green Light Readers edition 2005
Green Light Readers is a trademark of Harcourt, Inc., registered in the
United States of America and/or other jurisdictions.

Library of Congress Cataloging-in-Publication Data
Eaton, Deborah J.
My Wild Woolly/Deborah J. Eaton; illustrated by G. Brian Karas.
p. cm.
"Green Light Readers."
Summary: A boy discovers an imaginary animal in his backyard, but his mother
does not believe it is there.
[1. Imaginary creatures—Fiction. 2. Play—Fiction. 3. Imagination—Fiction.]
I. Karas, Brian, ill. II. Title. III. Series: Green Light reader.
PZ7.E1338My 2005
[E]—dc22 2004021933
ISBN 0-15-205148-1
ISBN 0-15-205147-3 (pb)

A C E G H F D B
A C E G H F D B (pb)

Ages 5–7
Grade: 1
Guided Reading Level: F
Reading Recovery Level: 9–10

Green Light Readers
For the reader who's ready to GO!

Five Tips to Help Your Child Become a Great Reader

1. Get involved. Reading aloud to and with your child is just as important as encouraging your child to read independently.

2. Be curious. Ask questions about what your child is reading.

3. Make reading fun. Allow your child to pick books on subjects that interest her or him.

4. Words are everywhere—not just in books. Practice reading signs, packages, and cereal boxes with your child.

5. Set a good example. Make sure your child sees YOU reading.

Why Green Light Readers Is the Best Series for Your New Reader

● Created exclusively for beginning readers by some of the biggest and brightest names in children's books

● Reinforces the reading skills your child is learning in school

● Encourages children to read—and finish—books by themselves

● Offers extra enrichment through fun, age-appropriate activities unique to each story

● Incorporates characteristics of the Reading Recovery program used by educators

● Developed with Harcourt School Publishers and credentialed educational consultants

Daniel's Mystery Egg
Alma Flor Ada/G. Brian Karas

The Fox and the Stork
Gerald McDermott

Moving Day
Anthony G. Brandon/Wong Herbert Yee

Try Your Best
Robert McKissack/Joe Cepeda

Animals on the Go
Jessica Brett/Richard Cowdrey

Lucy's Quiet Book
Angela Shelf Medearis/Lisa Campbell Ernst

Marco's Run
Wesley Cartier/Reynold Ruffins

Tomás Rivera
Jane Medina/Edward Martinez

Digger Pig and the Turnip
Caron Lee Cohen/Christopher Denise

Boots for Beth
Alex Moran/Lisa Campbell Ernst

Tumbleweed Stew
Susan Stevens Crummel/Janet Stevens

Catch Me If You Can!
Bernard Most

The Chick That Wouldn't Hatch
Claire Daniel/Lisa Campbell Ernst

The Very Boastful Kangaroo
Bernard Most

Splash!
Ariane Dewey/Jose Aruego

Skimper-Scamper
Jeff Newell/Barbara Hranilovich

Get That Pest!
Erin Douglas/Wong Herbert Yee

Farmers Market
Carmen Parks/Edward Martinez

My Wild Woolly
Deborah J. Eaton/G. Brian Karas

Shoe Town
Janet Stevens/Susan Stevens Crummel

A Place for Nicholas
Lucy Floyd/David McPhail

The Enormous Turnip
Alexei Tolstoy/Scott Goto

Why the Frog Has Big Eyes
Betsy Franco/Joung Un Kim

Where Do Frogs Come From?
Alex Vern

I Wonder
Tana Hoban

The Purple Snerd
Rozanne Lanczak Williams/Mary GrandPré

A Bed Full of Cats
Holly Keller

Did You See Chip?
Wong Herbert Yee/Laura Ovresat

Look for more Green Light Readers wherever books are sold!